Mr. Stuffy's Uniform

A Children's Story of Comfort for Troubled Times

D0815658

BARBARA DAVOLL

Illustrations by
DENNIS HOCKERMAN

REGULAR BAPTIST PRESS
1300 North Meacham Road
Schaumburg, Illinois 60173

MR. STUFFY'S UNIFORM
© 2002
Regular Baptist Press • Schaumburg, Illinois
1-800-727-4440
All rights reserved
Printed in U.S.A.
RBP5268 • ISBN: 0-87227-716-X

For the children
whose lives have been forever changed
because of the terrorist attacks
on the World Trade Center,
the Pentagon, and United flight 93—
September 11, 2001.

Barbara Davoll is an award-winning, best-selling writer of children's books, including the Christopher Churchmouse series and the Molehole Mysteries series. She and her husband, Roy, live in Schroon Lake, New York, and they minister to children in partnership with Word of Life and with the Association of Baptists for World Evangelism. Barbara and Roy have two married children, who, with their spouses, are involved in ministry. The Davolls have six grandchildren.

Dennis Hockerman has collaborated with Barbara on the illustrations for all her books. He is an accomplished children's artist. In addition to children's trade books, he has illustrated textbooks, magazines, greeting cards, and games. He and his wife and three children live in a suburb of Milwaukee, Wisconsin.

Contents

The Phone Call

Morning recess was over, and Mrs. Ward's fourth graders trooped in noisily after playing a rousing game of kick ball. As they came into the classroom, they noticed the principal talking seriously to their teacher.

"Uh oh, looks like someone's in trouble," whispered Anna Miller to her friend, Shelby.

"You've got that right," agreed Shelby as they took their seats next to each other. "Look at Mrs. Ward's face. She looks sort of pale. Wonder what's up?"

As the principal left the classroom, Mrs. Ward walked to the front of the room and called the class to attention.

"Students, I have just learned that we will dismiss school in thirty minutes. There has been a terrorist attack in New York City. It seems best to allow you to go home to be with your parents at this time. We don't have much information yet, but the school secretaries are calling your parents to see if they are home. If your parents aren't home, we will provide care here until they can come for you. You may gather your things and prepare for dismissal. I will soon have a list of the children who will stay. The buses will arrive shortly. There is no reason for alarm. All is being done to assure our safety."

Hands flew up all over the classroom, and Mrs. Ward answered as many questions as she could. One boy asked where the attack took place.

"It seems the World Trade Center was hit, Steve. We don't know the extent of the damage yet. Probably by the time you get home, your parents will have more information. I know this is difficult, but I can't answer any more questions until we know more. Now you need to prepare for dismissal. Many of your parents are already waiting, and the buses will arrive soon. You will have an extra two days for your science project. Please take your reading books and also prepare for your spelling test on Friday. You will be notified when school will resume. Shelby Baxter, may I see you for a moment, please?" Shelby glanced over at Anna as she went up to Mrs. Ward's desk. Anna could see the worry on Shelby's face.

"Your mother called a few minutes ago, Shelby," Mrs. Ward said. "She wants you to go home with Anna Miller and stay at her house. She will call you there."

"Is Dad okay?" Shelby asked with concern in her voice.

"We don't know too much, honey. Your mother will call you," responded the teacher, giving Shelby a hug.

Anna and Shelby sat together on the bus. "I hope my dad is okay, Anna," said Shelby. "He works in Tower Two."

"Mrs. Ward said there was no cause for great alarm," soothed Anna. "I'm sure he is fine."

It was a short ride to the neighborhood where the girls lived. As they headed up the long driveway that led to Anna's home, both girls were deep in thought.

"Maybe you'll get to stay for supper tonight," said Anna, trying to be cheerful.

"That would be fun," agreed Shelby. "The teacher said Mom would call me. I hope she calls soon."

"Let's hurry!" encouraged Anna. "Maybe Mom knows something more by now."

As the girls neared the house, Anna's mother was waiting for them at the door.

"Shelby's mom said she was supposed to come home with me," explained Anna as her mother greeted them with hugs.

"I know, honey. Maureen called me. I'm so glad you girls are home. Come on in to the kitchen. There's the buzzer for the cookies in the oven." Mrs. Miller hurried toward the kitchen to remove the cookies. The girls followed, chucking their book bags in the hall.

"What's up, Mom? Do you know why we were dismissed early? The teacher said there was a terrorist attack in New York City."

After removing the last cookie to the wire tray to cool, Mrs. Miller came over and gave the girls a group hug. Anna and Shelby stood still, waiting for her to speak. "I've been praying for just the right way to tell you girls. Something has happened today—and Shelby, your dad was involved."

Shelby's heart began to pound as she stared at Mrs. Miller. "This morning" she continued, "two planes were hijacked and crashed into the office buildings where your father works. Your mother has left her office to see if she can hear some word about him. Many people were injured, and some are missing. We have not yet heard about your dad. Your mom will call as soon as she knows more."

Mrs. Miller put her arms around Shelby as the little girl began to cry. "I'm so sorry, honey."

Anna began to cry too, and Mrs. Miller gathered both girls in her arms. "Try not to worry, Shelby. I'm sure your mother will call soon. Now, why don't we pray for your daddy's safety?" Shelby nodded and tried to stop crying. But she continued to sob as Mrs. Miller prayed. "Dear Heavenly Father, we are concerned just now for the safety of Shelby's dad. Would You please help him wherever he is and protect him? Help Mrs. Baxter, too, as she tries to find out more about him. Please comfort her and Shelby as they are worried about him, and please help all of the people who are hurting. Thank You, God, for loving us and being our helper. And thank You, too, for cookies and milk that always seem to make us feel better. Amen."

Giving the girls tissues for their tears, Mrs. Miller said, "Now let's have these cookies while they're still warm, shall we?"

Neither of the girls felt much like having cookies, but they had to admit that the warm treat, along with Mrs. Miller's prayer, did make them feel some better. As they sat around the table, Shelby asked in tears,

"Who are these hijackers? Why did they do this?"

"They're terrorists—really bad guys," answered Anna's big brother, Tom, coming into the kitchen and grabbing a handful of cookies. "They don't care at all about taking lives or dying themselves. Who knows why?"

Shelby put her head down on the table and began to sob. "It isn't fair. My dad didn't do anything to them. Why should he have to suffer?"

Just then the phone rang. Shelby lifted her head and tearfully looked toward the phone.

Something to think about . . .

1. Have you ever wondered why bad things happen to good people? Maybe you've thought, like Shelby did, that something "just wasn't fair."

All of us think that sometimes, don't we? It is wise to learn that life isn't always fair. As much as all of us want things to be pleasant and right, sometimes things happen that we just can't understand.

2. What are some things that have been really hard for you to understand? Has someone you loved died? Are your parents divorced?

Those are very difficult things to understand.

When hard times come, we need to go to God's Word for help and truth. Psalm 46:1 and 2 and Isaiah 41:10 are wonderful, comforting verses.

"God is our refuge and strength, A very present help in trouble. Therefore we will not fear, Though the earth be removed, And though the mountains be carried into the midst of the sea."

"Fear not, for I am with you; Be not dismayed, for I am your God. I will strengthen you, Yes, I will help you, I will uphold you with My righteous right hand."

A prayer to pray . . .

Lord Jesus, sometimes I really am afraid, especially when hard things come. Please help me to trust You with my life and help me to know You are taking care of me and of those I love. Thank You, Lord, for loving me and caring for me. Amen.

The Answer

Mrs. Miller, who had been comforting Shelby when the phone rang, answered quietly. "Oh yes, Maureen . . . yes . . . she's here. Is everything all right? Oh, thank the Lord! Here she is," she said, handing the phone to Shelby.

Shelby took the phone with tears streaming down her face. "Mommy, are you all right? Where's Daddy? Oh, Mommy . . . I'm so glad. Will he have to stay in the hospital? How long? Yes, I will . . . I love you, Mom. Tell Daddy I love him too. Here's Mrs. Miller."

The little girl burst into tears again and handed the phone to Mrs. Miller. "My daddy got out just as the building crashed. He's hurt his leg, and Mommy is with him at the hospital," she said between sobs.

Anna and Shelby hugged and cried together, and even Anna's brother, Tom, who usually paid no attention to the girls, hugged them. Mrs. Miller talked a bit longer to Shelby's mother, getting more details.

When she hung up, Mrs. Miller's own face was wet with tears. She gathered the girls into her arms and hugged them. "We need to thank the Lord for keeping your daddy safe, Shelby. Many people are still missing and some are badly injured. It has been a terrible thing."

"Father," she prayed, "we are *so thankful* for the wonderful way you kept Shelby's dad safe today. We pray for all of the others who are missing—and for the families who are waiting to hear about them. We don't understand why this has happened, Lord, but we pray for the wicked men who helped these men do this evil. Please help them to learn about You, and help those of us here in the United States to forgive them. Amen."

Mrs. Miller wiped her eyes and said, "Your mom says the hospitals are jammed, and doctors are treating the badly injured people first. Your father will have to wait for treatment, but they are keeping him comfortable until they can work with him. He will have to stay in the hospital overnight so they can be sure he is all right. The police have closed all of the bridges and tunnels in and out of New York City, so your parents won't be able to get out here to the suburbs until those are opened up—maybe tomorrow or the next day. The traffic is terrible in the city, so the hospital has fixed a bed for your mother in your father's room. She will stay right with him. She says you may stay with us until they get home."

"Can we watch the news about it on TV, Mrs. Miller?" asked Shelby, trying to stop crying.

"Ummm, probably not now, honey. I think it will only upset you further. Why don't you change into some playclothes of Anna's and go outside to play?"

"We can work on our tadpole project," said Anna. She was so relieved to know Shelby's dad was all right, and her voice sounded happy.

"You two are tadpoles yourselves," teased Tom.

Anna wrinkled her nose at him as they went to get changed. "What a brother!" she complained.

Later that evening at supper the children had many questions for Mr. Miller.

"Daddy, will the terrorists come here?" asked

Anna. She paused with her fork in the air, waiting for his answer.

"I don't think so, Anna," answered Mr. Miller.

"Naw! We're not important enough for any terrorists to come here," was Tom's answer. "Besides, if they did, we'd stop 'em!" he boasted.

"If that's the case, why didn't the police stop them?" asked Shelby.

"They didn't know they were coming, silly. We know now, and we'll be watching for them; right, Dad?" asked Tom.

"Well, yes, Tom. I'm sure the United States government will work diligently to make sure we are all more on our guard. However, the threat of terrorism is very hard to combat. It's worldwide, you know."

"That really makes me afraid!" cried Anna. "Is there no place to be safe?"

"Oh yes, Anna. There is a place of safety. It is right in the arms of God—if you are trusting Him. Psalm 23:4 says, 'Yea, though I walk through the valley of the shadow of death, I will fear no evil; For You are with me.' "

"You see, honey, the Bible tells us in Proverbs 21:31 that 'deliverance is of the LORD.' Our safety is up to Him. He has planned all the days of our lives from the time we are born. The Lord knows the day He will take us home to Heaven. The Bible says, 'It is appointed for men to die once.' Until the day of our 'appointment,' the Lord will keep us in safety. And even when we die, if we know Him as our Savior, He will walk beside us and welcome us home to Heaven."

Anna understood what her dad was saying, but she still had some questions in her mind.

 Something more to think about . . .

1. Perhaps you, like Anna, have thought that there is no place where you can be safe. What can you do when you have doubts about your safety?

It is so good to find comfort in the Word of God. Listen to these wonderful verses.

> "He who dwells in the secret place of the Most High Shall abide under the shadow of the Almighty. I will say of the LORD, He is my refuge and my fortress; My God, in Him I will trust. . . . He shall cover you with His feathers, And under His wings you shall take refuge. . . . For He shall give His angels charge over you, To keep you in all your ways" (Psalm 91:1, 2, 4, 11).

2. If God is our protector like those verses say, does that mean you will never get hurt or have something bad happen to you?

That is a very good question. Although God's Word promises that He will be with us, we know that sometimes terrible things happen. In Romans 8:28 we read,

> "And we know that all things work together for good to those who love God, to those who are the called according to His purpose."

When the worst does happen, if we are trusting Christ as our Savior, we can be sure that whatever happens will be for our good. That is God's promise to us, and we can trust Him to keep it.

Bad Thoughts

After supper the Millers got out some games, and the girls tried to beat Tom at Sorry.

"Sorry!" he taunted. "No can do! I'm the winner," he gloated.

"Tommy, I think you cheated on that last move," said Anna with a gleam in her eye.

"Are you kidding?" he laughed. "If I can't beat you without cheating, I'd be pitiful."

"Okay, kids, time to put it away," said Mr. Miller as he started to pick up the pieces of the game. "It's time for bed."

"Come on, Shelby. You can wear my nightie," said Anna kindly. "I'll let you cuddle Mr. Stuffy, my teddy bear, tonight." Anna picked up the bear from a chair where he was sitting. "I used to sleep with him every night," she said, handing him to Shelby. "He always helped me a lot when I had a hard day." Anna could tell that Shelby was still worried about her parents.

When the girls were ready to be tucked in, both Mr. and Mrs. Miller came to pray with them. Shelby sat propped up in bed beside Anna. Holding tightly to Anna's bear, Shelby began to sniffle and cry during Mr. Miller's prayer. Mrs. Miller sat beside her on the bed, holding her close.

"It will be all right, dear," she soothed after Anna's dad finished praying. "Your folks will be home just as soon as possible. It will seem better in the morning."

Shelby wiped her eyes and nodded. "I know, Mrs. Miller. But I just keep thinking bad thoughts. What if my daddy hadn't gotten out of that building? What if it had smushed down on him like a lot of the others that didn't get out? And what about the men Dad works with? I keep wondering about them and if they got out in time. I just keep thinking about it."

Mr. Miller looked at Shelby kindly. "I understand,

Shelby. Would you like me to read some verses to help you?"

Shelby sniffed back her tears and nodded. Mr. Miller picked up Anna's Bible and began looking for the verses. "Let's see—here we are in Psalms again. Listen to Psalm 94:18 and 19: 'If I say, My foot slips, Your mercy, O LORD, will hold me up. In the multitude of my anxieties within me, Your comforts delight my soul.'"

"Here are some helpful verses in the book of Philippians. These verses are so comforting and tell us what to do when we have bad thoughts. 'Be anxious for nothing, but in everything by prayer and supplication, with thanksgiving, let your requests be made known to God; and the peace of God, which surpasses all understanding, will guard your hearts and minds through Christ Jesus' " (Philippians 4:6, 7).

"Those are wonderful verses, Jack," said Mrs. Miller. "God's Word is so comforting in difficult times. I think maybe it would help Shelby and Anna to pray and give thanks. We have so much to thank God for, even though many others are still hurting from this incident."

"Anna, would you like to pray first? Then maybe

Shelby," invited Mr. Miller. Both girls nodded in agreement.

Anna prayed, "Dear Jesus, I thank You that I know You as my Savior, and I thank You for keeping me safe. Thank You, too, Jesus, for keeping Shelby's dad and mom safe. Help us to trust You. Amen."

As Shelby began to pray, the tears were still in her voice. But she grew stronger as she talked to the Lord. "Dear God, thank You for keeping my daddy safe—and Mommy too. Help Daddy not to hurt too much. Please let Mom and Dad get home soon. I'm so glad our family knows You. But God, I pray for all those other people they are trying to find. Please help them to get out. And help me to trust You. I love You. In Jesus' name, amen."

"Do you think you can sleep now, Shelby?" asked Mrs. Miller, kissing her goodnight.

"I think so," murmured the tired little girl, whose day had been so difficult.

"Just squeeze Mr. Stuffy," said Anna sleepily. "He always helps me when I have bad thoughts or dreams. I wish all those people who got hurt knew Jesus and had a Mr. Stuffy."

More help for bad thoughts . . .

What can you do when you pray and give thanks and you still have bad thoughts and you still worry?

Philippians 4:8 tells us what to think about so we can have peace.

> "Finally, brethren, whatever things are true, whatever things are noble, whatever things are just, whatever things are pure, whatever things are lovely, whatever things are of good report, if there is any virtue and if there is anything praiseworthy—meditate on these things."

Reading God's Word and thinking about it will help take the bad thoughts out of our minds. Here's something you can do. Find several verses that talk about God's protection. Write each verse on a separate 3" x 5" card. When you finish writing the verses, use a paper punch to make a hole in the top left corner of each card. Place the cards on a key ring so you can easily read and memorize the verses. Get out your Truth Cards anytime you are discouraged and have bad thoughts. Here are some verses to get you started.

> "Oh, satisfy us early with Your mercy, That we may rejoice and be glad all our days!" (Psalm 90:14).

"For we do not wrestle against flesh and blood, but against principalities, against powers, against the rulers of the darkness of this age, against spiritual hosts of wickedness in the heavenly places. Therefore take up the whole armor of God, that you may be able to withstand in the evil day, and having done all, to stand" (Ephesians 6:12, 13).

The Next Day

The next morning Anna and Shelby were awakened by the singing of birds and by the warm sunshine streaming through the window.

"Look Shelby! It's going to be a beautiful day, don't you think?" asked Anna with a happy voice.

"Umm, I sure hope so," replied Shelby with a still-sleepy yawn and stretch. "Maybe Mom and Dad will come home today," she said with excitement, letting her feet hit the floor with a happy bounce.

"Will you get ready for school at your house?" questioned Anna.

"I don't think so. I guess I'll just go get my clothes

and come back here to dress," Shelby replied, gathering up her stuff. "It's so early, I'll just run across in your nightie."

"Better hope you don't see the paperboy," giggled Anna. "He goes to our school, you know. He would make a big deal of seeing you that way."

"If I see him, I'll be sure to tell him it's your nightie," laughed Shelby.

"Do you want me to go with you?" asked Anna.

"Would you?" replied Shelby with a little catch in her throat. "I know it will be lonely at the house without Mom and Dad."

"Sure I will. I'll tell my mom and dad we're going. And just in case the paperboy rolls by, here's my other robe. I almost forgot I had another one."

As the girls left the house, the quiet suburb was just coming awake. The early fall sun shone down on the lawn, making the dew sparkle like diamonds. "Let's hurry," laughed Anna. "We're getting our slippers wet."

"I'll just be a minute," Shelby said as she felt for the key in its hiding place under a rock in her mom's flower garden. She swallowed a lump in her throat as she fit the key into the side door and saw the empty garage. Both cars being gone reminded

Shelby how close her father had come to death. Anna noticed her friend's sadness and suggested they needed to hurry.

The girls quickly packed Shelby's clothes and the other things she would need for school. As they passed through the kitchen, Shelby stopped before the little TV on the counter.

"Let's see what the news is saying," said Shelby, and before Anna could protest, Shelby flipped on the TV. The picture was the scene of the tragedy. The girls stood horrified as they watched firefighters, police officers, and others digging through the rubble. "The mayor of New York City has said that as many as 5,000 people may have lost their lives here," said the news announcer sadly.

"Mom said not to watch this, Shelby," said Anna, quickly turning off the TV and picking up her friend's suitcase. Shelby stood with her hands covering her face. Tears were falling as she said, "Lots of my daddy's office friends died there, Anna. The TV announcer says there may be thousands."

"I know," replied Anna, putting her arm around her friend and helping her leave the house. As the girls locked the door, Anna said, "We sure have a lot to be thankful for. At least your dad will be all right."

Shelby nodded her head and tried to stop the tears. "Come on, Shelby," Anna said cheerfully. "First one to my house gets to shower first."

Shelby, a better athlete than her friend, reached the house first and headed into the bathroom. While Shelby was in the shower, Anna began to make the bed. As she pulled back the covers, she picked up Mr. Stuffy, who was still snuggled down in bed where Shelby had left him.

Mr. Stuffy looked at Anna with his usual pleasant expression. "You never change, do you, Mr. Stuffy?" Anna placed him in his chair and gave it a little rock. Now that she was ten, she and Mr. Stuffy had a different relationship. He wasn't her constant companion as he had been when she was younger, but he still held a place of honor in her heart.

Saying that Mr. Stuffy never changed reminded Anna that Jesus never changes. Kneeling beside her bed, Anna thanked the Lord that He is always the same, and she asked Him to help Shelby and her family. When Shelby came out of the shower, Anna was writing some prayer requests in her journal.

Just then the phone rang. The girls looked at each other as Mrs. Miller hurried to answer it. "Shelby, it's your mother!" she called happily.

With a happy hug and smile from Mrs. Miller, Shelby ran down the hall to answer the phone. She was so glad to talk to both of her parents. Mr. and Mrs. Miller and Anna stood in the hall, listening to the happy phone conversation. Even Tom poked his sleepy head out of his door. "That's cool," he smiled and hurried to get dressed for school.

As Anna and Shelby climbed on the school bus, several of their friends asked about Shelby's dad. The girls were glad to tell them of Mr. Baxter's narrow escape from the falling building. It seemed as if everyone wanted to talk about what had happened. Anna was glad when they reached school because she noticed that all the talk was making her friend sad again.

When the girls got to school, Mrs. Ward, the teacher, asked the children to stand for a moment of silence to honor those who had lost their lives. Anna took the opportunity to pray silently, especially for the children who were affected by the tragedy.

At recess Shelby was the center of attention as all of the kids clustered around her, asking her how her dad had gotten out. Anna could tell that Shelby didn't want to talk about it. She knew it hurt her to even think about it. Anna was just about ready to tell the kids to change the subject when Mrs. Ward joined the group around Shelby.

"Why don't we play some kick ball," she suggested. "I'm sure Shelby has answered enough questions for now." As one of the boys went after the ball, Mrs. Ward gave Shelby a hug. "I know this has been a hard time for you, Shelby. I'm very thankful your dad is all right."

"Thank you, Mrs. Ward. I know the kids are just interested, but I thought I was going to cry if I had to tell that story one more time."

Mrs. Ward nodded understandingly. "You may have an extra day for your tadpole project," she offered. "I'm sure you didn't have much time last evening to work on it."

"Not much at all," admitted Shelby. "But I think I'll feel more like working on it tonight."

Something to think about . . .

1. Have you ever noticed that when something bad happens, the kids all want to talk about it?

Sometimes it is cruel to bring up subjects that are very painful to others.

2. What are some things you can do if a conversation is getting out of hand?

That's exactly right. You can change the conversation like Anna was going to do. Or you can suggest a diversion like Mrs. Ward did with the kick ball game.

3. Have you noticed the different times that the Millers and Anna prayed?

The first time was when they heard the very bad news. Then they prayed to thank the Lord for keeping Mr. Baxter safe. They prayed again before going to bed. And Anna prayed before going to school. The Bible tells about a man who loved God, Daniel, who prayed three times a day (Daniel 6:10). David wrote,

> "Evening and morning and at noon I will pray,
> and cry aloud" (Psalm 55:17).

The New Testament tells us to "pray without ceasing" (1 Thessalonians 5:17). *The most important thing you can do for a friend who is hurting is to pray for that friend.*

Something else to do . . .

Maybe you noticed that Anna was writing in a prayer journal. That is a neat idea! You might want to try that too. Get a blank journal or notebook. Write in it like you would write in a diary, only write your thoughts and prayers to the Lord. You might begin like this, "Dear God, I love You, and I want You to help me with my—."

Use a page in your prayer diary to write down the things you are asking from God, your requests. Leave a space to put the date when that prayer was answered. Then you can rejoice when you read your diary and see how God has answered and blessed you. Try to write in your prayer journal every day.

This is how a sample page might look. If you wish, you can write some requests right here.

Date	Prayer Request	Date Answered

Anna's Dilemma

The next evening at supper Tom asked, "Dad, what's going to happen? My friend Mark said his dad thinks we are going to war."

"Yes, son, it is very serious. When the plane crashed into the Pentagon, that was an attack on the highest military officials in our government. We cannot let this attack on our freedom go. We must try to stop these terrorists."

"Daddy, Nancy's father works for the government. He is at the Pentagon a lot. You don't suppose . . ." Anna let her voice trail off in a worried way.

"When I heard that the Pentagon was involved,

I called Nancy's mother," said Mrs. Miller. "Her husband wasn't in Washington when the crash occurred, but he has driven there today. Do you think we'll have war over this, Jack?" Mrs. Miller asked her husband.

"I'm afraid so, dear. The President is calling for the National Guard to be on alert, and the navy has already ordered its warships to stand by."

"Does that mean that Eddie Glen down the street will go, Dad?" asked Tom. "He's in the National Guard."

"He probably will, Tom. All of America is ready to defend our nation since so many people in our country have lost their lives. The President has called for a National Day of Mourning for prayer and remembrance on Friday."

"What's a . . . Day of . . . Mourning?" asked Anna. "Does that mean we'll have a prayer service in the morning?"

"To 'mourn' means to be sad, honey," explained Mr. Miller. "It is a day the country has set aside to remember the missing and dead. It's a time to pray and seek God's direction for the coming war action."

"Will we be excused from school?" questioned Tom.

"I believe so, Tom. It will be a very sober time for our country. The flags will fly at half-mast for several days. That means they will not be at the top of the flagpoles. Seeing the flags at half-mast will help us remember what has happened."

"Dad, I have another question for you," said Tom. "I think you know my friend Chad who's on the football team with me." Mr. Miller nodded his head. Indeed he did know Chad, who was a fine quarterback for the team.

"Chad's father thinks it isn't right for us to go to war," continued Tom. "He doesn't think we should repay evil for evil and have revenge killings. What do you think about that?" Tom asked earnestly.

Mr. Miller picked up his Bible from the bookcase behind the table and smiled with understanding. Some people in his office thought the same thing. "Why don't we talk about this question right now for our family devotional time? I think it would be wise to look at some Scripture verses to see what the Bible has to say."

The Miller kids and Shelby settled back in their chairs to listen as Mr. Miller leafed through his Bible to find the verses. "Here are some verses that explain why we have a government," he began. "Romans 13:1

and 2 say, 'Let every soul be subject to the governing authorities. For there is no authority except from God, and the authorities that exist are appointed by God. Therefore whoever resists the authority resists the ordinance of God, and those who resist will bring judgment on themselves.'"

"These verses are talking about the government," said Mr. Miller. "We follow our President and Congress not only because these leaders are elected by us, but also because they are placed over us by God."

"We are not repaying 'evil for evil' by declaring war on the terrorists," continued Mr. Miller. "That would be getting even, and that is wrong. What we *are* doing is defending ourselves. All through the Old Testament God led His people to defend themselves by making war on God's enemies. This war we will fight now is a war that is just and right, Tom. Listen to these next verses in that same chapter of Romans 13: 'For rulers are not a terror to good works, but to evil. Do you want to be unafraid of the authority? Do what is good, and you will have praise from the same. For he is God's minister to you for good. But if you do evil, be afraid; for he does not bear the sword in vain; for he is God's minister, an avenger to execute wrath on him who practices evil.'"

"I think I understand, Dad," said Tom thoughtfully. "I guess if we go to war to do something bad, like stealing territory from another country or something like that, it would not be a war that is just and right. But to defend ourselves from attack is okay. Is that it?"

"That's it, Tom. God has given me the right as your father and head of my family to defend and protect all of you. The same is true for government leaders. God has given them the right to defend and protect our nation from such vicious attacks as these."

After the Millers and Shelby had their supper, prayer time, and Bible reading, Tom settled down at the kitchen table to do his homework. Anna and Shelby had some work to do to finish up their tadpole projects. The teacher had said all the class could have another day to work on their projects. Dad turned on the television.

"Shelby, Anna, and Tom! Come listen to this. You too, Dorothy!" called Mr. Miller. The children and Mrs. Miller hurried to the family room.

"Look at this. Do you remember when there was

a bombing in Oklahoma City?" asked Mr. Miller.

The children and Mrs. Miller nodded. "Who could forget it?" she said.

"Do you remember how people from all over our country sent teddy bears to the children in Oklahoma City who lost their parents? Well, this report says that the children in Oklahoma City have gotten those teddy bears cleaned up and have written notes to tie around the bears' necks. The children of Oklahoma are now going to send bears to the children of New York."

"Oh, isn't that sweet," murmured Mrs. Miller, wiping her eyes with a tissue.

Anna stared at the television pictures of the children writing the notes and tying them around the bears' necks. One boy who was interviewed said into the microphone, "I just want to help somebody else like people helped me." The announcer explained that the boy's mother died when the federal building was bombed.

After the report ended, Anna went to her room. She picked up Mr. Stuffy and sat down on her bed. She held Mr. Stuffy to her heart, thinking hard about what she had just seen. "Is that something I should do, Mr. Stuffy?" she whispered, with a catch in her voice and tears in her eyes. Mr. Stuffy looked as wise and pleasant as usual, but he answered not a word.

 ## How can I help?

1. When terrible things happen, one of our first questions is, How can we help?

Our hearts go out to those in trouble, especially if we have been spared pain. When Anna saw how the children of Oklahoma City responded by sending their bears to the children of New York, she thought about her own precious bear, Mr. Stuffy. Should she send Mr. Stuffy to someone who was hurting and needed comfort?

Here are verses about God's comfort and how we may comfort others.

> "Blessed be the God and Father of our Lord Jesus Christ, the Father of mercies and God of all comfort, who comforts us in all our tribulation, that we may be able to comfort those who are in any trouble, with the comfort with which we ourselves are comforted by God" (2 Corinthians 1:3, 4).

2. God's Word teaches us that the bad things we experience can help us be more understanding when we see others who have similar trouble. That's what

"comfort those who are in any trouble" means in the verses above. Can you remember a time when you reached out to someone in trouble because you had once had that same kind of trouble yourself?

Anna's Decision

Three days went by before Shelby's dad came home from the hospital. The Millers planned a wonderful meal of celebration to welcome him home that day. The whole neighborhood rejoiced with the Baxter family.

Later that week a program on television honored the hundreds of firefighters, police officers, and emergency personnel who had lost their lives trying to rescue the people before the buildings collapsed.

Anna snuggled between her parents on the couch as they watched the program. She was still holding tightly to Mr. Stuffy. "Oh, Mom, those poor firemen and policemen!" Anna cried. Mrs. Miller patted her and pulled her closer in a loving way.

Tom, who was sitting on the floor in front of them, had been watching quietly. "Those policemen and firefighters were really heroes, weren't they, Dad?" Tom asked soberly. "I mean they were running into the buildings when everyone else was trying to get out. They sure were brave."

"Yes, Tom. Sometimes God gives ordinary men and women courage to do extraordinary things during times of great danger."

"Did all the heroes go to Heaven, Dad?" asked Anna.

"The heroes who knew Jesus as their personal Savior are in Heaven, Anna. A person does not go to Heaven just because he or she was brave or did brave things. I'm sure you remember what Jesus said in John 14:6: 'I am the way, the truth, and the life. No one comes to the Father except through Me.' All the heroes will be honored here on earth for their bravery and their death in the line of duty. I'm sure the government will give special awards to their families, as well."

The next news report showed soldiers from all over the country saying good-bye to their families. One wife stood by her soldier husband, who was holding their little baby. She said they would miss him greatly but they were proud he could serve his country as a soldier.

Tom shook his head sadly. "He may not come back. A lot of our soldiers will die, won't they, Dad?"

"Yes, Tom, there is always that possibility in war. We must really pray as our country sends men and women into harm's way."

"Would you want me to go if I were old enough?" Tom questioned.

"It would be very difficult for us to let you go, son," said Mrs. Miller with a sigh. "But we would be proud to have you serve God and our country. We can trust God for whatever He has for your future."

"You know, Mom and Dad, I've really been thinking. It would be fine to serve the Lord in the army. I mean, because I know Jesus as my Savior, I could help the other soldiers who don't know about Him."

"Yes, son, the Lord needs young people who are true Christians to serve in the armed forces. I'm glad you're thinking about your future. It is a long time from now if you would go, but it's wise to think ahead. And we can certainly pray for all the people going off to fight for our country, especially for those we know, like Eddie Glen."

"I've been thinking a lot too," added Anna. "Since I heard what the children in Oklahoma City are doing with their bears, I've been thinking I'd like to send Mr. Stuffy."

"Wow, Anna, you'd better think some more about that," laughed Tom. "How would you get to sleep at night? You've had him since you were a baby. I don't think you could get along without him."

"I could too, Tom Miller. I don't sleep with him every night anymore. And besides, I know Jesus now and don't need a bear to go to sleep. I can trust Jesus as well as you can. I'd like to send Mr. Stuffy to someone who doesn't have a mom and dad to help him, maybe like a soldier."

"Ahh, for cryin' out loud, Anna. No soldier wants an ole bear. They've got more to do than play around with toys," jeered her brother. "They're fighting a war."

"Tom, don't discourage Anna," replied Mrs. Miller. "If she wants to do something to help, let's encourage her. We'll help you send him wherever you want, sweetie," she added.

"I'm sorry. I didn't mean to put a wet blanket on her idea," apologized Tom. "Give me that ole bear, sis," he said, reaching around for Mr. Stuffy.

"Hey, ole Stuffy!" he continued, taking the bear from Anna and talking to him. "What do you think about it? You wanna go to war?" Mr. Stuffy looked as pleasant as he could.

"Ya gotta fix Stuffy's ear, Annie," Tom continued. "It's about ripped off. The army won't accept anything like that."

"I'll help you sew him," offered Anna's mom.

"And I'll help you take him to the Red Cross tomorrow," offered her Dad.

"Ya wanna use my red, white, and blue ribbon from the medal I won?" suggested Tom generously. "You could tie a little note around his neck like the kids did in Oklahoma."

"Sure," answered his sister, taking Mr. Stuffy and heading to her room. Things were moving a little too quickly for Anna. Once the bear's ear was sewn and the note was written to tie around his neck, Mr. Stuffy would be ready to go. He would be ready, but was Anna ready to say good-bye to him? She knew that would not be easy.

 **More questions for thought . . .**

1. Would you like to be a hero?

All of us look up to heroes, don't we? And all of us like to receive awards for what we have done. The police officers, firefighters, and emergency personnel who gave their lives trying to rescue other people were certainly heroes and deserving of awards.

But the greatest gift we can receive is the free gift of eternal life that is offered by Jesus when we become children of God.

> "And this is the testimony: that God has given us eternal life, and this life is in His Son. He who has the Son has life; he who does not have the Son of God does not have life" (1 John 5:11, 12).

Our status in Heaven is not based on what we do on earth, but on accepting the work Jesus did for us when He was on earth—dying on the cross for our sins.

For those of us who are God's children, the greatest award is awaiting us—eternal life with Jesus in Heaven. He is the hero of all heroes, for He took our sins upon Himself and paid for them with His own blood. Not only is He preparing a home in Heaven for us (John 14:2, 3), but He will give crowns to those who love Him and wait for Him to return.

"Finally, there is laid up for me the crown of righteousness, which the Lord, the righteous Judge, will give to me on that Day, and not to me only but also to all who have loved His appearing" (2 Timothy 4:8).

2. Who is your hero? Is it Jesus Christ, the greatest hero of all? Is He your Savior and Lord? You can receive Him today!

"If you confess with your mouth the Lord Jesus and believe in your heart that God has raised Him from the dead, you will be saved" (Romans 10:9).

A Sad Good-bye

On a beautiful Saturday morning late in September, the Miller family was up early. Anna sat at the kitchen table, writing on a little heart-shaped card with a marker. Beside her on the table was Mr. Stuffy and the red, white, and blue ribbon her brother, Tom, had given her. Anna's mom sat nearby. She had just finished sewing the bear's ear that needed repair.

Mrs. Miller glanced over at Anna, who was resting her head on her hand. Her forehead was wrinkled, and she was obviously thinking hard. "How are you coming with the message for the card, honey?" asked Mrs. Miller.

"So far I have 'Dear Friend' written. It's hard to know what to say. The card is so small. I've already written two that won't work because I wrote too big," sighed Anna. "What do you think I should say, Mom?"

"I think you should decide that yourself, Anna. But if I were you, I would try to be loving and encouraging."

Anna picked up the marker and began again. Printing in small, neat letters she wrote:

Dear Friend,
This is Mr. Stuffy, my good friend, who always helps me when I am afraid.
I will pray for you both to be safe.
John 3:16.

When she finished writing the card, Anna read to her mother what she had written. "Do you think that's okay, Mom?" she asked.

"I think it's fine. Here's a paper punch. Just make a little hole in the center and then string it on the ribbon. That's it," said Mom, helping Anna pull the ribbon through. "Now tie it with a double knot like we do your sneakers." Together they got Mr. Stuffy ready to go.

"Hey! Ya got that ole bear ready to go?" asked

Tom, as he and his dad came in from raking leaves. He looked down at the bear lying on the table. Stuffy was wearing his usual sweet expression. "Ready to go for your last ride, Mr. Stuffy?" he said jokingly. When Tom saw that Anna was ready to cry, he tousled her hair and grabbed an apple from the basket on the counter. "I'm outa here," he said quickly. "Gotta get to football practice. Have a nice trip, Stuffy. You show those soldiers over there how to do it."

"He looks very nice, honey," said Mr. Miller approvingly, looking at the bear. "I like what you put on the card. And you can hardly see the stitches in his ear. Well, let's get him on his way. We should be back by noon," he informed his wife, giving her a kiss.

Mrs. Miller gave Anna a hug and then she gave Mr. Stuffy a kiss. "Do well, Mr. Stuffy, dear," she said. "You have been part of our family for a long time. We'll miss you a lot."

Tears came to Anna's eyes as she took the bear from her mother. Going back to her bedroom, Anna closed the door and looked at Mr. Stuffy.

"It's time to go, Mr. Stuffy. I know you don't understand it all, but I just want to thank you for being my good friend for so long. I will always love you and have you in my heart. But I have Jesus and my mom and dad to watch over me. I think maybe you can help someone else who might need you more." Giving him a hug, Anna ran to the car, and they were on their way.

When Mr. Miller and Anna arrived at the Red Cross building, they were met by a kind lady who helped them find the area where donations were being accepted for the war effort. Anna saw men and women packing boxes of clothing—warm socks and underwear—and also personal items such as toothpaste and soap.

"Do you have a special place for this very special bear?" asked Mr. Miller, pointing to Mr. Stuffy. A lady looked up from a list she was making and saw Anna standing quietly, holding Mr. Stuffy.

"We sure do. I'll be glad to see he gets to just the right person," she said. "Do you want him to go to a little girl or a boy?" she asked Anna.

"Oh, please, ma'am, I told Mr. Stuffy he would go to a soldier. Could you do that?"

The lady smiled and looked at another lady, who was making a list. "Put this bear with things going to the soldiers," said the first lady as she winked.

"Right away," said the other lady with a little

salute to Anna. "Come along, little bear. You are on your way to a big adventure."

The last Anna saw of Mr. Stuffy, he was sitting on top of a box of socks and underwear.

With a little salute toward her furry friend, Anna took her dad's hand and walked away—but not before she saw what she thought was a tear on Mr. Stuffy's face. She couldn't be sure because of the tears in her own eyes.

Some thoughts about saying good-bye

1. It is always hard to say good-bye to someone we love, isn't it?

In Anna's case that someone was just a little stuffed bear, but to Anna he was very real. It is even harder to say good-bye to people we love, and especially when someone dies. It is easier to say good-bye if the people we love are Christians. Then we know we will see them again in Heaven—if we are sure we know the Lord ourselves.

2. Do you know the verse Anna put on the little card around her bear's neck?

John 3:16 is probably one of the best-loved verses in the Bible.

> "For God so loved the world, that he gave his only begotten Son, that whosoever believeth in him should not perish, but have everlasting life" (KJV).

This verse assures us that if we believe in Jesus and if we trust in His death on the cross to save us from our sins, then we can have everlasting life.

God Bless America

As Anna and her dad drove home from the Red Cross, Anna noticed flags *everywhere*. It seemed that nearly every store displayed a flag. Some flags were flying in front of the buildings, and some were hanging in windows. "Wow, Dad! Look at all the flags!"

"Isn't it great! I just love to see it," responded Mr. Miller.

As Mr. Miller and Anna went under an underpass, they noticed a long banner hanging down that said in huge letters, "God Bless America!" A large flag was displayed beside it.

"Look at that," said Anna pointing to the banner. "It says, 'God bless America.' People are thinking a lot more about God since the attacks, aren't they?" she observed.

"Yes," agreed her dad. "Sometimes it takes a tragedy to help people remember that there is a God."

"Dad, there's something I've been wondering about since the attacks. We know that God is a God of love. But I've been wondering why He would allow this to happen? Why would He allow all of those people to die? Some of the kids at school said God was punishing America for our sins. Is that true?" she asked.

"Well, honey, it is true that we as a country have not remembered God as we should. That is sin, and we know that the Bible tells us that 'the wages of sin is death.' That means death is a payment for sin. However, the Bible also tells us in 2 Peter 3:9 that God is 'longsuffering toward us, not willing that any should perish.' That means God is full of love and mercy and is very patient with us and our sinning ways."

"I've heard our pastor say that God has blessed America," stated Anna. "And the President always says, 'God bless America,' when he closes his speeches. Did God choose *not* to bless us on the day of the attacks?" Anna was worried. Mr. Miller could tell she had been thinking a lot about this matter.

Mr. Miller thought before he responded. He wanted to say just the right thing. "There is a verse in the Bible that says, 'Blessed is the nation whose God is the LORD.' We have been greatly blessed of God, Anna, because our forefathers founded our nation on the truths of God's Word."

"I still don't understand why God caused these attacks to happen in our country," said Anna. "Has God stopped blessing us?"

"No, dear, God has not stopped blessing us. And He did not 'cause' the attacks. Evil is present in the world. The Bible says the Devil is always prowling around, looking for someone to destroy. God has allowed him to have some power for a little while, but not forever. Our God will have the victory eventually. Those men who attacked our country were filled with evil. They caused the suffering, not God. But think how God blessed us even in the attacks."

"Our whole country was not bombed or destroyed," he continued. "And many many thousands of people escaped from the bombed buildings. As bad as the attacks were, we are still a strong nation. And look at all of these flags and the signs of hope and encouragement. We are more united than ever. God has really blessed us, honey, in spite of the presence of evil. And He will continue to bless us, but how much He will bless us will depend on how much our nation follows Him."

Just then Anna and Mr. Miller passed a billboard with a picture of Jesus overlooking the map of the United States. Each state on the map contained a smaller picture that was symbolic of some great blessing in that state. At the top of the map were the words "God Bless America—the land of the free and the home of the brave."

"Oh, look, Daddy! 'The land of the free and the home of the brave!' "

"That's us, sweetheart. We are blessed—and we are free—and we will be brave."

Mr. Miller had a lump in his throat as he looked at Anna. He could see in her eyes that hope was returning.

Just then the traffic slowed to a stop. A convoy of army trucks and soldiers was crossing in front of them. Several policemen were directing the large number of men in their trucks. It was one of the army reserve units from the area. The soldiers were obviously on their way to report for duty and serve their country.

Taking Anna's hand, Mr. Miller prayed, "God bless us and make us brave."

Some more thoughts about God's blessings . . .

1. Have you wondered why God doesn't stop evil? Why does He allow it to exist?

When the Lord created Adam and Eve and placed them in the Garden of Eden, He allowed them to make a choice. God told Adam one tree had forbidden fruit. It was the tree of the knowledge of good and evil. The Lord made it clear that Adam and Eve should not eat of that tree's fruit. Adam and Eve made a very bad choice. They deliberately chose to do what God had forbidden. Adam and Eve chose to sin against God. And that very day sin came into God's perfect world, and sin has been part of our world ever since. (You can read about Adam and Eve's sin in Genesis 3.)

2. God did not want His creatures to be robots. He gave us the opportunity to make choices. Some people choose great evil rather than blessing. Many times the evil that men and women do touches good

people—innocent people—who do not deserve to suffer. That does not mean God caused the evil or the suffering. Because of mankind's sin through Adam and Eve, we have sin in the world. But God has given us a choice:

> "See, I have set before you today life and good, death and evil" (Deuteronomy 30:15).

> "Choose for yourselves this day whom you will serve" (Joshua 24:15).

3. Look at this beautiful passage about God's blessing. It is in Psalm 33:12–22.

> "Blessed [happy] is the nation whose God is
>   the LORD,
> And the people whom He has chosen as His
>   own inheritance.
> The LORD looks from heaven; He sees all the
>   sons of men.
> From the place of His habitation He looks
> On all the inhabitants of the earth;
> He fashions their hearts individually;
> He considers all their works.
> No king is saved by the multitude of an army;
> A mighty man is not delivered by great
>   strength.
> A horse is a vain hope for safety;

Neither shall it deliver any by its great
    strength.
Behold, the eye of the LORD is on those who
    fear Him,
On those who hope in His mercy,
To deliver their soul from death,
And to keep them alive in famine.
Our soul waits for the LORD;
He is our help and our shield.
For our heart shall rejoice in Him,
Because we have trusted in His holy name.
Let Your mercy, O LORD, be upon us,
Just as we hope in You."

Ribbons and Prayers

The United States continued the war buildup, moving troops and supplies to areas where they could defeat terrorists. Young people from all over the country considered joining the armed forces, and many of them did. The Millers' neighbor Eddie Glen was preparing to leave home.

One Friday evening in late October a candlelight prayer service was held in the city park. Anna and her family, along with Shelby's family and many others, attended the service. They held their lighted candles and prayed as the mayor read a list of people from their community who would be leaving to serve in some area of military service. Anna and

Shelby stood together, their candles making a warm glow on their faces. All over the park the little lights shone bravely in the darkness. At the end of the service the entire group of people sang "God Bless America." Anna had tears in her eyes and a lump in her throat as she thought of the soldiers who would be going into danger. This was a very serious time.

On Saturday the town had a huge parade to honor the people who would be leaving that day. Again Anna and Shelby stood together, waving their flags as the soldiers marched by.

"There's Eddie Glen!" said Anna excitedly. "Praying for you, Eddie!" she yelled. Like a good soldier Eddie didn't look her way, but Anna saw a smile come across his face.

That evening after supper Anna sat at the kitchen table. Taking pieces of red and white and blue ribbons, she was trying to make a pin she could wear to show that she was praying for America.

Coming over to the table, Mrs. Miller laid a spool of ribbon in front of Anna. The ribbon on the spool was red, white, and blue. "Try this ribbon, honey. I think it will be easier than trying to get three pieces of ribbon to stay together."

By twisting the ribbon and putting a small pin on it, Mrs. Miller had made a special little patriotic pin in no time.

"That's neat, Mom. Let's make one for all of us," suggested Anna. "And I know Shelby would like one and so would her mom and dad."

Mom and Anna became so involved making ribbon pins that they continued until they had used up all the ribbon.

"Mom, I've been wondering what I can do to help the war. Do you suppose I could make more pins and give them to our neighbors and the kids at school? Maybe that would help them to remember to pray for the soldiers. Can we get some more ribbon?"

"I think so," answered Anna's mom. "The ribbon isn't that expensive. Maybe we could get some little pins at the craft store so they would all be alike."

"I would really like to do that," said Anna enthusiastically. "Maybe Shelby and some of the girls could come over Monday and help. Could you get the ribbon by then?"

"I'm sure I can. Let's try to get it together for Monday," agreed her mom.

"May I call Shelby and tell her? Then she could help me call some of the girls to see if they can come."

Mrs. Miller agreed. Before Anna went to bed that night, she had several girls lined up to help with the ribbons.

When Tom saw the ribbons the next morning, he thought they were cool. "How are you going to give them out, Anna?" he asked.

"I don't know. I hadn't thought of that," admitted his sister.

"How about I get some of the guys to help. If you make enough of 'em, we can deliver 'em with our bikes," he suggested.

"Hey! What if we got some baskets or something for you to put the ribbons in? We could make some little signs to put on the baskets," Tom suggested further. "The signs would say the ribbons are prayer reminders about the war. Then we guys could deliver one to every restaurant and business in town. The restaurants and businesses could put the baskets by their cash registers. Then people would see the ribbons when they pay their bill at the cash register and take one. People would love to take 'em if they're free. You girls can keep making more, and we will keep the baskets filled each week."

Anna looked at her brother with surprise on her face. *Is my brother actually offering to help me and my girlfriends do this?* she wondered.

"Hey! What'cha lookin' at?" he asked in his usual Tom way. "Ya think boys don't care about the war? Sure we do," he asserted with a determined look on his face. "We'll help ya!"

Anna looked at her mother, who had heard their conversation. Mrs. Miller had a huge smile on her face. "Will wonders never cease?" she remarked.

Some thoughts about prayer . . .

1. What was the first thing the Millers did when they knew their country was in trouble?

If you said "prayed," you are right. Wherever they were—at home, in the car, or even in public, such as at the candlelight service in the park— they prayed. Probably they had read these verses in 1 Timothy 2:1 and 2:

> "Therefore I exhort first of all that supplications, prayers, intercessions, and giving of thanks be made for all men, for kings and all who are in authority, that we may lead a quiet and peaceable life in all godliness and reverence."

These verses tell us who to pray for and what to pray for: (1) for all people; (2) for the things people need; (3) for kings and leaders; (4) for all those in authority; (5) that we may worship and respect God.

2. Did you notice in our story how Anna was always looking for something to do for her country?

Anna loved America, and she wanted everyone to know it. She also loved the Lord, and she wanted people to know that too. This Bible verse talks about letting people know we are people of faith.

> "Be ready always to give an answer to every man that asketh you a reason of the hope that is in you with meekness and fear" (1 Peter 3:15, KJV).

Anna thought her lapel ribbons were a gentle way she could let people know that she was praying for America. Do you pray for our country and our President and other leaders? If you haven't prayed before, will you start now?

The Celebrities

Anna and Tom had never been busier. When their friends heard about the prayer ribbons, they all wanted to help. Anna and the girls met twice a week at Anna's house to make the ribbons. Mr. and Mrs. Miller had decided, after praying about it, to contribute to the project for the kids by buying the ribbon. Mr. Baxter, Shelby's dad, had decided to buy the little baskets that held the ribbons. He also helped by making some signs on his computer to attach to the baskets.

After school Tom and his friends delivered the ribbons to the businesses in town. In no time at all it seemed everyone in town was wearing a little

patriotic prayer reminder made by Anna and her friends.

One evening in November when the girls were hard at work making the pins, Mrs. Miller turned on the news on television. "Girls! Come here!" she called from the family room. "Look at this!"

The news report was chilling. An undercover reporter had taken pictures in the training camp of the terrorists in a far-off country. The pictures showed the intense training that the terrorists endured. They were running up and down a high sand dune in the boiling hot sun. Small boys, some no more than nine years of age, were running in a line behind them. The boys were being trained at that young age to do exactly what the men did. The little boys even had uniforms just like the men.

Mrs. Miller and the girls looked at the television in silence. What they saw made them sick. Imagine *children* being trained to do such hideous things and *children* being called upon to give their lives to do evil. When the report ended, the girls went back to making the ribbons. But they had a new determination.

Anna couldn't seem to forget the pictures of those children. At supper the Millers talked it over.

Mrs. Miller and Anna explained to Mr. Miller and Tom what they had seen.

"Man! It just makes ya mad, doesn't it?" said Tom. "To think they are ruining those kids' lives."

"It makes me want to do more to help," said Anna quietly. "I wonder if other kids in our country would like to help. I've been thinking we should form some sort of a club where kids all around our country could share ideas about how to help. Maybe we could have a Web site and encourage other kids in the country to make ribbons and to pray for America."

"That's a good idea," agreed Anna's father. "If you come up with a name for your club, I'll look into getting the Web site set up."

"I already have a name," said Anna excitedly. "What about the 'Brave and Free Kids Klub'?"

Tom gave a low whistle of approval. "That's a great idea, sis. I like the name. We could have a newspaper, and all of us could contribute patriotic stuff to encourage kids to pray and care about the war cause. Let's do it!"

That was the beginning of the Brave and Free Kids Klub. Before the year was over, kids from all over the country were online with Anna and Tom.

A whole network of encouragement was going out over their Web site, which they called the Freedom Kids Network.

One day the phone rang in the Millers' kitchen. Anna was absorbed in her homework at the kitchen table. "Well, what a surprise!" said Mrs. Miller as she hung up the phone. "That was someone from the local television station. The station wants to send a reporter to interview you and Tom and some of the other kids from your club. Looks like all of you have become celebrities. It seems there is a great interest in what you are doing, and other towns are interested too. The reporter wants to come here next week to interview all of you."

Anna stared at her mom in surprise. She had no idea that an even *greater* surprise was in store for her as well.

Some things to think about . . .

1. The pictures on television of the young boy terrorists were disturbing to Anna. Why do you think Anna was sad?

One reason may be because the children were being taught to hate and to do evil. Their entire lives would be ruined by the lies they were taught, and eventually they would end up giving their lives for an unworthy cause. In the twisted thinking of the terrorist leaders, terrorism is a noble thing. They had convinced themselves and the children that if they had to sacrifice their lives for their cause, they would be pleasing their god.

2. The word "sacrifice" is an interesting one. The dictionary says "sacrifice" is an "offering of something precious" or "accepting loss for a cause or an ideal." During wartime, a soldier is asked to sacrifice for his country. He gives up his freedom for a time so that he may fight, and he has to be under the authority of his commanding officers. Sometimes he is required to sacrifice his life. Many soldiers have fought bravely and have lost their lives fighting for their country.

The Bible says in John 15:13,

> "Greater love has no one than this, than to lay down one's life for his friends."

When you read this verse, who do you think made the greatest sacrifice of all? You are right if you said Jesus Christ. He gave His life as a sacrifice for the sins of the world. What great love He had for you and me!

3. The Bible gives us another thought about sacrifice in Romans 12:1:

"I beseech you therefore, brethren, by the mercies of God, that you present your bodies a *living sacrifice,* holy, acceptable to God, which is your reasonable service."

When we think of sacrifices in the Bible, we usually think of animals that were killed. But this verse makes it clear that God wants us to offer our lives to Him as *living* sacrifices. He wants us to be holy and pleasing to Him and to give our bodies to Him for His use. He is worthy of any sacrifice we make for Him because He gave His life as a sacrifice for us.

The Surprise

Anna hurried off the school bus and started up the driveway. Then she remembered she should get the mail from the mailbox. Pulling down the door to the mailbox, Anna whistled. The box was jammed full. In the months since she and her brother had formed the Brave and Free Kids Klub, they had received lots of letters from kids asking how they could start a club in their towns.

Anna walked slowly up the driveway, looking through the mail as she went. Suddenly she stopped and stared down at the *Prime News Magazine*, which was stuck in with all the letters. On the cover of the national news magazine was a picture of several

soldiers dressed in their fatigue uniforms. They were standing around a Humvee. The thing that made Anna gasp was that Mr. Stuffy was sitting upright on the hood of the vehicle! She could hardly believe her eyes! Anna knew it was her bear because he was still wearing the heart-shaped card she had lettered and tied around his neck. And she could see that his ear was showing even more wear since she had left him at the Red Cross almost a year ago.

"Oh, my dear Mr. Stuffy, what are you wearing?" she asked, staring at the picture. "Why Mr. Stuffy, you have on a uniform! Where did you get that?"

Anna burst into the house yelling, "Mom! Come quickly!" Mrs. Miller hurried down the stairs and met Anna in the hall.

"What's wrong, honey? Are you all right?"

Anna laid the other mail on the hall table and held up the magazine for her mother to see. "It's Mr. Stuffy, Mom. He's got a uniform!"

Mrs. Miller took the magazine and sat down on the step to look at it. "Why, Anna, it surely *is* your Mr. Stuffy. And doesn't he look adorable! Look at that little uniform. It looks just like the one the soldiers are wearing!"

"I know," said Anna with excitement in her

voice. "I've gotta call Shelby!" Anna ran into the kitchen to call her friend.

Mrs. Miller paged through the magazine until she found the article that told about Mr. Stuffy and the soldier who had received him in the box from the Red Cross. The soldier's name was Sergeant Michael Norton. He was from Nebraska and was a member of the Special Forces. He served in one of the groups that made parachute jumps into enemy territory. The article recounted some of the brave and daring things his company had done in fighting the war against terrorism.

When Anna returned to her mother, Mrs. Miller was wiping her eyes. "Read the article, Anna. It begins here," said her mom, obviously touched by what she had read. "There is even a close-up picture of the little card you tied around Mr. Stuffy's neck."

Anna sat down beside her mother on the step and took the magazine. She read the article about how Michael Norton and his soldier buddies had made Mr. Stuffy their mascot and how they had sewn a little uniform for him out of one of their old fatigues. The article said Michael always took Stuffy, along with a small Bible, in his backpack when he was going into danger. The soldiers in the platoon had been greatly helped by some child's gift.

When Anna finished reading the article, her mom gave her a big hug. "Now we know the name of the soldier, Anna. We must pray for him and his buddies. The article says they still face many dangers."

"Oh, Mommy, let's pray now, shall we?" asked Anna with tears in her voice.

Anna and her mother were still praying when the phone rang. Anna continued to pray silently. When Mrs. Miller came back, she reported that the call was from the television reporter who was coming to interview Anna. Mrs. Miller told the reporter about the news article, and she said she would read it before she came and then ask Anna some questions about it.

"They want to come tomorrow after school, Anna, so they can air the program Friday night. Will that be all right with you?" asked Mom.

"Sure," answered Anna, who was overwhelmed by it all. "I mean, I really didn't do much but take my bear to the Red Cross."

"That was a lot, my dear. It was a sacrifice on your part. A lot of Americans will be encouraged by it," answered Mrs. Miller.

"Didn't Mr. Stuffy look handsome, Momma? He was sitting there on the Humvee like a little soldier," said Anna proudly. "I'm so proud of him for doing his part so well."

"Yes, Anna. You and Mr. Stuffy are making us all proud Americans," answered her mom. "Now let's get some supper ready for some other proud, hungry Americans who will be home soon," laughed Mom.

 Something to think about . . .

1. Anna said she was "proud" of Mr. Stuffy. Do you think she was prideful in a wrong way?

Sometimes we use the expression "I'm proud of you," but "proud" is not exactly what we mean. I think Anna meant she was thrilled that Mr. Stuffy was being used of the Lord in just the way she had hoped. And I think Mrs. Miller was "proud" of her Anna in the same way. She meant she approved of the way Anna was conducting herself, because she knew that what Anna was doing was bringing glory to the Lord. Right there in the news magazine was the little card Anna had tied around Mr. Stuffy, which said she was praying for the soldier and which included the John 3:16 Scripture reference. Anna was being a good witness.

2. *Did you notice that Anna didn't sign her name to the card she tied around Mr. Stuffy's neck? Why do you think she didn't?*

Perhaps Anna thought it wasn't too important for someone to know her name. Anna was not full of pride, and she wasn't thinking of receiving any thanks or glory for herself when she gave the best thing that she had to help the war effort. She was only thinking of how she might be able to help somebody else.

3. *What do you have to give that could help others?*

The Bible tells us in Titus 3:1 that we should "be ready for every good work." What are some things you might do to help your country when it is in crisis? Not everybody can start a Brave and Free Kids Klub, but each of us can do something. What can you do to show that you are a loyal American? In James 3:13 we read,

> "Who is wise and understanding among you? Let him show by good conduct that his works are done in the meekness of wisdom."

Never forget that "God so loved the world, that he GAVE his only begotten Son." What can you give so that others may hear of Him?

The Purple Heart

The next day when Anna and Tom came home from school, the television station's news van was parked in the Millers' driveway, along with an equipment truck. Big cables were running into the house, and cameramen were busily setting up for the interview of the Miller family. The reporter began the interview by asking Anna to tell the story of Mr. Stuffy. Then Tom told about delivering the ribbons and about how he and his sister had started the Brave and Free Kids Klub. They also described their Web site.

The reporter concluded the interview by saying, "You've just seen how some ordinary American kids have made a difference in their community and the world."

After the interview aired on the Friday evening television news, things around the Miller home returned to a regular routine. Anna and her friends continued their efforts. They added weekly prayer meetings to their busy schedules so they could pray for the soldiers and particularly for Sergeant Michael Norton and his buddies, who had received Mr. Stuffy.

One Saturday nearly a year after the Millers' television interview, a car pulled into their driveway. Tom, who was washing the Millers' car, was the first to greet the two soldiers who emerged from the car.

"Is this the Miller residence?" boomed the friendly voice of the soldier who had been driving.

"Sure is," answered Tom, wiping his soapy hands on his jeans and walking forward to greet the soldiers. As he did so, he noticed that the other soldier used crutches because one of his legs was missing. The soldier was wearing a huge smile though and asked, "Is Anna home? My name is Michael Norton, and I have something for her."

Tom's mouth dropped open, and he stared in disbelief. "I'll . . . I'll . . . get her right away. Come on in," Tom stammered, running to find his sister.

Anna came into the living room, and the soldiers introduced themselves. Anna took one look and ran over to the crippled soldier. "Oh, Sergeant Norton, we have been praying for you," she said, giving him a careful hug.

"I know you have, little lady," answered Michael. "I know you have."

"How did you find me?" asked Anna, who was still in shock at seeing Sergeant Norton in her living room.

"Your television station tracked me down through the news magazine and sent me a clip of your interview. All of us soldiers watched it. We've even seen the Web site of the Brave and Free Kids Klub."

"Oh," said Anna with a gasp. "You mean way over wherever you were?" Anna sat down on the couch as Mr. Miller seated Michael comfortably in the chair opposite her.

"Yes, Anna. I just had to find you and tell you how much your Mr. Stuffy meant to me and my buddies, and I wanted to return him to you." Michael patted a cardboard box that the other soldier gave him. The box looked like a carrying case and said, "Caution! Bear inside!" The box even had little air holes like an animal carrying case would have.

Anna was staring at a special medal on Michael's

uniform. "I see you've noticed Michael's Purple Heart, Miss Anna," said the other soldier, whose name was Greg. "He just received that yesterday from the government."

"Michael saved our lives, Miss Anna. When we dropped in on the enemy that day, there were just four of us. Mike took the worst of it all, but even when he was injured himself, he crawled out and pulled two of us back to safety. Johnny didn't make it, sad to say."

"No, he didn't, but he received the Lord as he was dying, Anna," interrupted Michael. "All of that was because of the little note you tied on Mr. Stuffy, with John 3:16 on it. You see, I used to go to Sunday School when I was a kid. My mom gave me a little Bible when I entered the service. So when Mr. Stuffy came to us, I knew how to find that verse, and I found a whole lot more to help all of us."

"Mike helped us a lot by reading the Bible to us, and so did your Mr. Stuffy," said Greg.

"You see, he was in my backpack that day we almost didn't make it," explained Michael. "When the mortar shell went off, the backpack was blown apart, and Mr. Stuffy almost lost his bad ear. But we sewed it back on, and then Greg made him a little Purple

Heart. We decided Mr. Stuffy needed one, too, because he encouraged us all and helped us to find the Lord."

Michael hobbled over to Anna as she carefully removed Mr. Stuffy from the box.

"They tell me I won't be able to go back to the war, Anna," continued Michael. "Maybe when I've healed more, I can find something else to do for my country. But right now the doctors say I need a rest, and I thought Mr. Stuffy needs to have a rest too. Maybe he can encourage kids here in the States to stay brave and free and do all they can for God and their country."

Anna took her battered little bear, who was wearing the Purple Heart bravely on his uniform. His ear was stitched, not as neatly as when he left, but it was attached. And his smile was just the same. "Welcome home, my dear Mr. Stuffy," said Anna with tears in her eyes. "Welcome home! And well done!"

Remembering . . .

It was heartwarming to hear the story of Mr. Stuffy and how he helped the soldiers. Sometimes the most ordinary things can be used to help others.

In the story of Anna and Mr. Stuffy we have learned a number of truths that will help us as we live in our world—a world that can sometimes be very dangerous. Let's review those truths.

1. We learned that things are not always fair but that God's Word is the truth we can depend upon when bad things happen.

2. We learned that God is our protection and has planned all the days of our lives. He has also appointed the day of our death, and until then we are safe in Him.

3. We learned that we can have peace by asking God to keep our hearts and minds and also by thinking good, honorable, and true thoughts.

4. We learned that the best thing we can do when someone is hurting is to pray for that person.

5. We learned God uses the troubles we have had and allows us to comfort others who may face the same things we have faced.

6. We learned that Jesus Christ is the greatest hero of all and that He offers us the gift of eternal life. We receive eternal life by accepting Jesus as our Savior.

7. We learned that saying good-bye to someone we love is difficult, although it is easier if we know Jesus as our Savior. When a friend or loved one who knows Jesus dies, we know we will see that person in Heaven someday.

8. We learned that God does not cause evil. Evil things are the result of sin, which started when the first man and woman disobeyed God by eating of the tree of the knowledge of good and evil.

9. We learned that we should pray for all people, for people in authority, and for ourselves.

10. We learned that the greatest sacrifice or gift we can give is to lay down our life for a friend. Jesus laid down His life for us so that we may be saved from our sins.

11. We learned that we need to be willing to give of ourselves for others even as God gave His Son for us.

12. Did you notice that when Anna received Mr. Stuffy back again she said, "Welcome home! And well done!"? Did you know that Jesus will say those very words to each of His children who has done his or her best for Jesus? (See the story Jesus

told in Matthew 25:14–23.) If you know Jesus as your Savior, you can be working for Him now. Then you will hear Him say, "Well done!" when He welcomes you home to Heaven. I want to hear those words, and I'm sure you do too. That welcome gives us a really great goal to work for, doesn't it?

We hope you enjoyed reading about Mr. Stuffy.
You won't want to miss his Web site:
www.mrstuffy.org
You'll find games, puzzles, coloring pages, crafts,
and some ideas about how you can share
God's message with the people around you.